Table of Contents

Meet the Characters

Ick

Crud

Miss Puffy

Bob

Mrs. Martin

Book 6

Ick and Crud

Happy Halloween

by Wiley Blevins • illustrated by Jim Paillot

RED CHAIR •PRESS•

Funny Bone Books

and Funny Bone Readers are produced and published by
Red Chair Press LLC   PO Box 333   South Egremont, MA 01258-0333
www.redchairpress.com

About the Author

Wiley Blevins has taught elementary school in both the United States and South America. He has also written over 60 books for children and 15 for teachers, as well as created reading programs for schools in the U.S. and Asia with Scholastic, Macmillan/McGraw-Hill, Houghton-Mifflin Harcourt, and other publishers. Wiley currently lives and writes in New York City.

About the Artist

Jim Paillot is a dad, husband and illustrator. He lives in Arizona with his family and two dogs and any other animal that wants to come in out of the hot sun. When not illustrating, Jim likes to hike, watch cartoons and collect robots.

Publisher's Cataloging-In-Publication Data

Names: Blevins, Wiley. | Paillot, Jim, illustrator.
Title: Ick and Crud. Book 6, Happy Halloween / by Wiley Blevins; illustrated by Jim Paillot.
Other Titles: Happy Halloween | Funny bone books. First chapters.

Description: South Egremont, MA: Red Chair Press, [2019] | Summary: "It's Halloween, the day for spooky ghosts and scary cats! There is plenty of action as Bob tricks Ick and Crud for a Halloween treat."

Identifiers: ISBN 9781634402620 (hardcover) | ISBN 9781634402668 (paperback) | ISBN 9781634402705 (ebook)

Subjects: LCSH: Friendship--Juvenile fiction. | Halloween--Juvenile fiction. | Dogs--Juvenile fiction. | CYAC: Friendship--Fiction. | Halloween--Fiction. | Dogs--Fiction.

Classification: LCC PZ7.B618652 Ich 2019 (print) | LCC PZ7.B618652 (ebook) | DDC [E]--dc23   LCCN: 2017957082

Printed in the United States of America
1018 1P CGBS19

"**B**oo!" yelled Crud.

"Ruff! Woof! Ruff! You scared the doggie bones out of me," said Ick.

"It's that time of year," said Crud.

"You mean pumpkins with bad teeth? Witches? And kids dressed as ghosts?"

"Yes," said Crud. "It's Halloween."

Ick shivered. "Halloween has too many ghosts. I don't like ghosts. They live in attics. And they eat little dogs."

"I'll protect you, buddy," said Crud.

Just then Bob walked in holding two boxes. On each was written: *Dog Costume.*

"Uh-oh," said Ick.

"Not this year," said Crud. "I'm not letting him dress me up like a hot dog again."

"You had it easy," moaned Ick. "Bob put me in a buggy last year. I had a baby rattle! Kids screamed and fainted when they saw me."

"Well, this year will be different," said Crud. "Stick with me."

"Like bubblegum," said Ick.

I Look Boo-tiful

"Come, Crud," called Bob. Crud acted like he didn't hear. "Crud!" yelled Bob again. "Come!"

"Not gonna do it," whispered Crud.

"Me neither," said Ick. "We're stuck together like bubblegum." Just then Bob scooped up Crud. And took him into the next room. "Nice sticking like bubblegum," yelled Crud. "You're next." Ick paced back and forth. And forth and back. Until...

a big white blob floated into the room.

"AAOOOHH! A ghost! I knew it!" yelled
Ick. He dashed under a table. And used
his nose to stop.

"AAAGGGHH!" yelled Ick. "My nose.
My nose! A ghost broke my nose."

"It's me, buddy," said Crud. Ick stared
at the white blob. It had four fat paws
under it.

"Take it off! Take it off!" yelled Ick.

Crud waddled to the big mirror. "I
think I look boo-tiful."

"Where there's one ghost, there's more,"
said Ick. "Take it off!"

"You're next," said Bob. He waved for Ick to follow him. "Oh, no," said Ick. "I'm too young to be a ghost. I'm too cute to be a ghost. I'm too...too...alive."

Ick darted under a chair. He slid on his belly. Then he grabbed onto the chair leg. "Save me, Crud! Be like bubblegum!"

Bob pulled and tugged. Ick's paws slipped off one by one. Pop! Pop! Bob scooped him up and carried Ick into the next room. "Hang in there, Buddy," said Crud. "No need to boo-hoo about it."

In a few minutes, Ick crawled back. A big wig wiggled on his head. "What am I?" he asked.

"You look like a poodle," said Crud. "A poodle who ate a rainbow."

Bob plopped something big and red on Ick's nose. "Oh," said Crud. "I think you're a clown."

"AAAGGGHH! Clowns are scarier than ghosts. Take it off. Take it off!" Ick spun in a circle. He flipped. He flopped. And when he stopped..."Ahhh-choo!" The nose shot off.

Bob grabbed it. He stuck the nose on Ick a bit tighter.

"Ahhh-choo. Ahhh-choo." The nose shot off again. "I think you're allergic to clowns," said Crud.

"I think so, too," said Ick. "What does ah-ler-jik mean?"

"Never mind," said Crud.

Meeting Cleopatra

By evening, Ick and Crud still had their costumes on. Outside the wind whipped the leaves up and down. And around and around. "Time for a quick walk," said Bob. "Let's go to the park."

"Not dressed like this," said Crud.

"No way," said Ick.

"Now!" said Bob. He snapped on Crud and Ick's leashes. And plopped the two down on the sidewalk.

"Hurry," said Crud. "Before you-know-
who sees us." He tugged on the leash. Just
then something moved above them. It let
out a piggy squeal.

"I will if you will," whispered Ick. Crud
and Ick looked up.

Mrs. Martin peeked over the fence. Her black witch's hat bent in the wind. Miss Puffy curled around her neck. She wore a crown with blue and gold jewels. "Who is she supposed to be?" said Ick.

"Don't ask," said Crud.

"I am Cleopatra," said Miss Puffy. She licked her paws like royal lollipops.

"Cleo-who?" asked Ick.

"The queen of Egypt," said Miss Puffy. "I float up and down the Nile River. I rule all the land. Everyone must bow down to me." She stared at Ick. "Bow now!"

Ick dipped his head. But a little too fast. He rolled to the left. Then to the right. And rolled right into Crud.

Miss Puffy hissed a laugh. "Your turn," she said. And looked at Crud.

"Not gonna happen," said Crud.

He tugged on the leash. "Come on, Bob," he barked. "The park can't be worse." Crud and Ick pulled Bob down the street. Around the corner. Around another corner. And into the park. A new sign hung on the entrance.

BIG BARKIN' HALLOWEEN PARADE

But Ick and Crud didn't see it.

Costume Contest

"Look at all the kids," said Ick. "Tiny vampires. Mini princesses. And dads who look bored."

"Remember last year?" asked Crud. "When Bob gave out treats."

Ick licked his lips. "Yes and yum. I'd bark, wait for the drop, then grab the treats."

"You ate a lot!" said Crud.

"Enough for a week," said Ick.

"You were sick for a week," said Crud.

"Good times," said Ick.

Bob led them through the crowd.
Crud wiggled and wagged. Ick wagged
and wiggled behind him. Bob stopped at
a big stage. On it sat dogs. Frog dogs.
Dinosaur dogs. And dogs in dresses.

"Hold the doggie door," said Ick.
"What is this?"

"A bad dream," said Crud.

"Am I dreaming?" asked Ick.
He blinked his eyes really hard.

"No, buddy. This is a costume contest."

"You don't think...?" asked Ick.

"Yes," said Crud. "Bob is entering us
in the contest. He tricked us!"

A man dressed as a milk carton came
on stage. A woman dressed as a cookie
stood beside him. "Welcome," said the milk
man. "Bring your dogs to the stage. The
judges are ready."

"And what do you win?" asked the woman. "The dog with the loudest claps gets all of this!" She pointed to a large silver cup. It was filled with doggie treats.

"Well, this changes things," said Crud.

"I will if you will," said Ick.

"We got this," said Crud.

Dog after dog walked across the stage.
The crowd laughed. The crowd clapped.
Louder and louder.

"Uh-oh," said Ick.

"We got this," said Crud.

Then it was their turn. "Just look cute,"
said Crud.

"That's how I always look," said Ick.

Crud rolled his eyes. "Follow me."

Bob led them on stage. Crud stood
on his hind legs. He howled "AHHOOH!"
The crowd clapped. Ick stood on his hind
legs. He tipped over. The crowd laughed
and clapped. But not loud enough.

"We need to do something more," said
Crud.

"What?" asked Ick.

"Try your flip," said Crud.

Ick wiggled to the side of the stage.
He took a little run. Then he flipped and
flipped. The crowd clapped louder. But not
loud enough.

"Do it again," yelled Crud.
Ick wagged his tail. Then he took
another run.

FLIP.
SPIN. CRASH!

Ick rolled into Crud. Crud rolled into Bob. Bob rolled into the big bowl. And the doggie treats spilled on top of them all. The judges looked mad. But the crowd went wild.

Ick poked his head out of the mess.
"Crunch! Crunch! We got the most claps,"
he said.

"Yes, we did," said Crud. "Let's go home.
And get out of these costumes."

"Come on Bob," they barked. "And don't
forget the doggie treats. It's going to be a
happy, happy Halloween after all!"